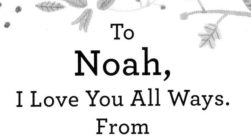

To
Noah,
I Love You All Ways.
From

....

Noah,

in case you ever wonder,
in the busy of our days,
exactly how you're loved by me,
I think you'll be amazed.

Noah,

I love you first thing wide-awake

and nighttime sleepy too,

and every minute in between,
I love all the ways of you.

Noah,

I love you storytelling tales
to friends all gathered round

and make-believing on your stage
in costume, cape, and crown.

Noah,

I love you
underneath the sea

and side-by-side on land.

I love you
riding piggyback

and walking
hand-in-hand.

Noah,

I love you grumpy and upset,
excited, sassy, mad.

I love you cartwheel joyful

and under-blanket sad.

Noah,
I love you far away from home

and cozy close to me.

I love you quiet
in your thoughts

and singing loud with glee.

Noah,

I love you playing peekaboo
and swinging feet to sky.
I love you face up in the sun,
watching clouds go by.

Noah,

I love you covered
in the snow

and splashing
in the rain.

I love you mighty
mountain strong

and achy sick
with pain.

Noah,

I love you moody mischievous,
bending rules your way,

because my love is longer still
than any longest day.

Noah,

I love you at the age you are
and every year you grow

into more the special someone
I forever want to know.

Noah,

top to bottom, inside, through:
you're the certain of my days.

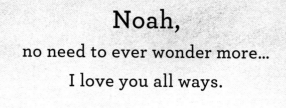

Noah,

no need to ever wonder more…
I love you all ways.

Noah,

draw a picture of your friends
and family that YOU love all ways!

Written by Marianne Richmond
Illustrated by Dubravka Kolanovic

This edition created by Bidu Bidu Books Ltd 2023

Put Me In The Story is a
registered trademark of Sourcebooks.
All rights reserved.

Published by Put Me In The Story,
a publication of Sourcebooks.
P.O. Box 4410, Naperville, Illinois 60567-4410
(630) 536-1104
putmeinthestory.com

Date of Production: September 2022
Run Number: 5026919
Printed and bound in China (GD)
10 9 8 7 6 5 4 3 2 1

MIX
Paper from
responsible sources
FSC® C117745
www.fsc.org

put me
in the story
Bestselling books starring your child!
putmeinthestory.com